BIG JOHN AND THE FORTUNE-TELLER

DUKE TATE

To my beloved wife, Wiphawan, my muse and inspiration. I love you with all my heart.

Look not at my outer form, but take what is in my hand.

— RUMI

CONTENTS

1

Big John stuffed the sausage in his mouth and downed it with a nice cold glass of Florida orange juice. Then he took a whole grand biscuit off his plate, split it in half, padded two big chunks of butter in the middle, and ate that too.

His mom, Susan Hoover, watched her son with utter bewilderment. John was like a trash compactor with food. He had always been a chunky child, but lately he was getting heavier every day. He just so happened to have one of those face and body types that looked good big, although he was pushing 260 pounds now at 5′8″—right on the line between "big" and "huge." Last summer, at fourteen years old, his parents had sent him away to fat camp for three weeks and he lost twenty-five pounds, but when he returned, nobody, not even his friends, could get used to his new look.

"Where did Big John go?" they all asked. "What should we call you now, Little John?" they said.

"No! Not Little John like the rapper, never call me that," John barked back.

Now at fifteen, he was in his prime and was having fun with food. Never full, all he ever really thought about was eating. One day, everyone said, he would probably be a chef: he found great pleasure in the preparation of food—although not always. He was an eater first, a cook second, and lately he had started to wonder if he might get a job tasting food for a living.

The one thing he hated about being 258 pounds was that the girls tended to go after guys with nice abs and built bodies—football and baseball players: jocks. The ladies didn't know he could give them a truffle shuffle if they wanted and make them all laugh. Nothing very funny about abs, he always thought.

If he had been skinny with his cleft chin and pug nose, he probably would have scored countless dates. He knew his nose could gain him some points down in the Deep South with a southern belle, but he was getting no glances from Maggie May, on whom he had the biggest crush ever. She had platinum blonde hair like a Swede, was 5′11″, and had the most penetrating blue eyes John had ever seen.

She liked this junior with Greek heritage named Bo. Tan with a long Roman nose, Bo was the polar opposite of Big John. John was Irish, but his hair wasn't red and he didn't "lobster up" in the LA sun like a true ginger—though he still burned all right, and it pissed him off.

Every night while lying in bed, John dreamed about Maggie May. While he was falling asleep, he played out scenarios in his mind of what could happen the next day at school. He would strut into class and see her talking with her girlfriends; she would turn and smile, staring back at him with those riveting eyes. And he would swagger over and say, "Hey babe," and they would start French kissing right there. It just had to be like that, or he would go crazy.

He always wondered whether she was named Maggie May after the Rod Stewart song or if it was just a coincidence. Many days, that song played on repeat on his phone, but he never let his buddies catch him listening to it. They knew about Maggie all right—he practically drooled over her whenever she walked by. Tall enough to be a model, soon she would be some kind of a superstar, especially since they lived in the city of dreams. Oh yeah, she would be hanging out at the Viper Room with all the super freaks, John thought.

Everyone said she was out of his league, but he didn't care. If there was one thing he had learned in life, it was that if you wanted something, you had to pursue it with all your will.

John had been bold already and slipped Maggie a note in English class, asking her if she liked turtles, just to be silly. She'd laughed, which he thought was pretty good. Everyone knew girls liked a funny guy and that six-pack abs didn't last on the court of true love. Perhaps Bo could bounce things off his stomach muscles, but who cared? To John, humor seemed to be the way to any girl's heart.

Big John and his buddies, The Zoo Crew, had a passion for all things Los Angeles. All three lived in the Santa Monica Canyon; some days, they skateboarded all the way down to Venice Beach where they pretended to be legends in Dog Town—the infamous area where the sport of skateboarding was invented. They liked to stop by Dog Town Café in Santa Monica on their way to Venice Beach and get coffee and a couple of burritos. Big John always ordered two or three and then ate everyone else's leftovers.

Lean and tall, Big John's best friend, Chris, was the best looking of the bunch. John was proud of how Chris could talk to any chick who passed by, no question. He also usually tossed John what he didn't eat, and that was a lot—and John was always searching for that full feeling. Sometimes, he felt like he had been put on this earth to live out an endless quest for satiety. He knew the exact moment it came, because his belly poked out a little and he felt very sleepy.

There was also something about his hands that made him eat. He often had this tingling feeling in them and sometimes they felt hot. Eating was the only thing that ever made the sensations go away.

Today, the Zoo Crew were in their Santa Monica Canyon hideout that was Mike's basement. Down there, in the dark realm, they had all their favorite Sega and Nintendo games and pin-up pictures of swimsuit models from the 80s. Mike was a slender Black basketball point guard with a big afro. Hanging on the entry to Mike's den was a poster of his hero, Shaft. It was their spring break, and the crew was spending their days wasting time.

"Hey big boy, give me the food!" Mike yelled.

"Don't call me that! You know I don't like being called that; I am just big boned, like a T. rex," John said.

"Well you took the Reese's Pieces and you won't give them back. Hand them over, pronto."

John gulped down half the king-sized bag of candy and passed it back to Mike.

"Dude what *is* this?" Mike crooned, holding the bag up. "You jerk! It's almost empty! Why don't you learn to control your stomach, John?"

"I need fuel, man. This body needs energy to run. You see how much I move around. That doesn't just happen—it takes sugar and meat and cheese."

"Big John can't help it, Mike; just leave him alone," Chris said. "Hey, so what are we going to get into today?"

"I don't know. I'm on a mission to find the perfect cooked French fry. We need to scope out every burger joint in the hood until we find the best fry in America," John proclaimed.

"That sounds fun," Mike said.

"Let's do it, boys!" Chris said.

At that, the trio headed out on foot to the closest diner: Sandra's on Montana Avenue in Santa Monica. Big John ordered two baskets of fries there, and the crew agreed to split them. They munched the greasy, skinless fries quickly.

"Aww, these suck! A four out of ten at best," Mike said.

"Yeah, no crisp to them at all. I can't even eat these," Chris said, pushing his away.

"Give them to me," John said, tossing a handful in his mouth.

"Hey Big John, I heard Maggie May is going out with that Bo guy now," Mike said.

"So? That stone fox is mine. What does Bo have that Big John don't?"

Chris and Mike laughed, then Mike shot back, "Are you serious, John? He has a nice mack ride, for one. A red BMW. And he's only like the coolest guy at Santa Monica High."

"Red? Isn't that a girl's color? What's he thinking, that he's some kind of hot chick or something? I don't know. Seems lame to me," John said.

"John's right, it's lame. Now if it was a red Spider Ferrari, that would be cool," Chris added.

The crew agreed to go to In-N-Out burger next, but the closest one was a long way on foot in Santa Monica. They all wished they were sixteen with drivers' licenses and cars.

Strolling through Palisades Park, which ran along the ocean in Santa Monica, the crew came across many homeless folks laying in the sun. Some were smoking marijuana, others just taking in the ocean breeze.

"Hey fat boy!" a voice yelled.

The crew looked up and saw the voice coming from inside a red BMW convertible. It was Bo, and who was sitting in the passenger seat but sweet Maggie May.

"Who you calling fat?" John yelled back.

"You, big boy," Bo said and laughed.

"I am not fat, I am large and in charge!"

"Whatever—come here," Bo said.

"Go over to him. See if we can get a ride to In-N-Out," Chris whispered.

"Yeah, go on with your bad self, John," Mike said.

John strutted over to the car like he owned the city. When he got to the passenger-side window, he flirted heavily with Maggie. Leaning in on the door, he asked her, "Hey babe, what you doing with this zero? You need to come hang out with the Zoo Crew."

"And go where, back to your parent's basement? You guys are losers, you can't even score a fake ID, and you don't have a car. You can't go anywhere," Bo said.

Maggie laughed and blushed a little, then said, "He's cute, Bo, leave him alone."

"He's about 280 pounds of fat blubber."

"Shut up, bad ass. At least I don't spend hours a day at the gym looking at my fanny, you big girl."

"So, what are you guys getting into?" Maggie asked, smiling. Her blue eyes were killing John.

"We are on a mission to find the best French fry in America, and since LA is the soul of America, we are trying to find the best fry in LA. In-N-Out is our next stop on the list."

She giggled. "That sounds fun."

"Listen Einstein, the closest In-N-Out is about three miles from here. Good luck walking your way in those

Chuck Taylors. You won't make it two miles before your mommy calls. Let's go, Maggie."

"No, wait. Do you guys need a ride?" Maggie asked, begging John to come.

"Don't mind if we do."

"No way, unless I get twenty bucks for the trip," Bo insisted.

"Twenty bucks? Come on, man!"

"Twenty bucks or you walk."

Big John took out a crisp twenty and handed it to Bo, then opened the back door of the Beemer and hopped in waving Chris and Mike over. The crew were off, spinning up Wilshire Avenue. With the top dropped, the air was cool and balmy. Maggie wore a periwinkle blue top that revealed just the right amount of cleavage; John drooled the whole way as he watched her in the rearview mirror. The trip was too short for John, and Bo kicked them out of his car at In-N-Out Burger.

"Hey, where are you guys going? Maybe we can roll with you?" Chris asked.

"Sorry bud, we're going to the Viper Room and then to a party in the Hills. No losers allowed."

Maggie smiled, watching John closely. "Maybe next time, guys."

Bo sped off and left the three boys standing there in the parking lot.

John raced in to get some food to fix his feelings about Maggie—his hands had started tingling again. He ordered two fries, one animal style for fun and one plain for the taste test. "Animal style" fries, a perennial In-N-Out favorite, were covered with grilled onions, secret sauce, pickles and a slice of cheese, emerging as a staple of the All-American California Teen diet—the average Angeleno couldn't survive longer than seven days without a healthy dose.

All three of the crew agreed In-N-Out had their vote for the best fries in America and they didn't need to continue the test anywhere else. But with exploration still in their veins, they agreed to make the hike to Venice.

3

The city's dusk fell on the boys as they wandered down to Main Street in Santa Monica. They decided to swing into their favorite spot—Dog Town Café—for some coffees. Big John ordered two grilled cheese sandwiches and a cold brew with three sugars. The crew plopped down in a corner and sipped their coffees while people-watching. An intellectual-looking man in grey heather sweatpants and a blue LA Dodgers hat sat down beside them with his Chihuahua and drank his coffee. A slinky brunette model walked in, alongside a guy with a staggering square jaw who was wearing a white tank top that oozed muscles.

"If you want to get with Maggie, you gotta look like that, Big J," Chris said, pointing to the guy.

John laughed. "I guess so, man. I don't know. What should I do? Tell me guys."

"Lose 60 pounds and get one of those ab rollers. Do that

about a thousand times a day and maybe you can carry her books to class," Mike said, squealing with laughter.

"That crap is not funny, Mike. Can I still eat if I do a thousand of those damn things?" John asked.

"Nope. You gotta eat chicken, lots and lots of chicken. Anything with feathers. And cauliflower," Chris said. "That's what I eat, bud, and look at me, I keep it sexy."

"I hate cauliflower, but I love me some Roscoe's, does that count?"

Chris and Mike bawled laughing. Roscoe's was LA's own fried chicken and waffle house.

"No bubba, you can't eat fried chicken, only grilled or broiled. And only the breast," Mike said.

"Aww man, I want some Roscoe's right now. I could go for a Sir Michael or a Lord Harvey. I'm getting hungry just thinking about it."

"What should we do tonight guys?" Chris asked.

"Viper Room," John muttered.

"No way, John," Mike said. "That is toast. I know what we can get into. Let's go down to Venice and see Madame Bernadette. My old man told me about her. My uncle went to see this Romany lady one day—wandered into her place off Oak Lane and she told him to buy three pieces of chocolate at a local chocolate store and give them to the first person he met. He did it, and this rich guy named Leroy who took the chocolates wrote him a check for $5,000. Leroy explained to my uncle that he had dreamed the night before to give a large amount of money to the first person he met who gave him something."

"*What?* That's the strangest thing I have ever heard," Chris exclaimed.

"I don't think I could buy chocolate without eating it," John said.

"We should go, guys. Madame will know how to get Maggie, John," Mike said.

"Okay, I am all in," John barked and shot up like soldier at attention.

"Okay, I guess we're doing this thing, but don't we need an appointment?" Chris said.

"No—she's a fortune-teller, not a lawyer; I would guess she takes walk-ins. Besides, how long could it take to peer into the murky unknown? Twenty minutes, tops."

4

adame Bernadette's cave was better than any office the crew had seen. It stank of sage and sandalwood, residue of the smoke from incense smeared over every surface of the room. Purple-blue velvet curtains lined the walls of her "seeing room." Jammed in the center of the tiny room was a circular table with a burgundy floral cloth thrown over it in true gypsy fashion. Madame waited there in her weird green French antique chair, greeting the boys with amber, eagle-like eyes that swarmed with a sea of mystery. She wore a patterned bandana and turquoise eyeliner on her tan French face and big circular earrings that looked like Gladiator shields. She was in her 40's and was not very beautiful.

Pointing directly to John with a long skeletal figure and gesturing for him to sit down in front of her, she crowed: "I know why you have come, Big John."

The boys were shocked by her admission.

"How do you know my name?" John asked.

"My sight doesn't lie. It's the ball. It tells me everything."

Madame put her bony hands around the magical ball, whirling with cloudy citrine, green, and blue smoke in a mist of fog and dismay.

"You want to marry this Maggie May girl," she said, dead serious.

"Yes—well, I guess so."

She swirled her left finger around the top of the ball while peering into the glass.

"You need time for that. But to be with her—that you could have," she said as she leaned back into the chair. "But you have to do something first."

"What's that?"

"You have to draw what you want with this pen," she said, laying a blue pen embossed with gold circular patterns down in front of him. "Remember, when you were younger, you used to love drawing. You even drew Maggie May once in the fifth grade in art class. She sat for you, but everyone made fun of you for being too artsy. Now draw like the wind —draw away the fat, my son."

"Aww shucks, the fat thing again! But I love to eat. I am Big John, that's what everyone calls me."

"Your choice. Losing the weight is the only way. This one you want, she likes appearances."

"Okay, I will try it."

"You can only eat half your appetite or less always. Or else all your weight will return the next day."

"Okay, what do I owe you?"

"Fifty dollars."

John reached into his pocket and tossed two crumpled

twenties and a measly ten on the table. The madame snatched it away and leaned forward, staring at him coldly.

"I see you fat, fatter than you have ever been, alone, living in your parent's house forever. That's what I see."

Her stare seared him like a piece of fish. John couldn't breathe; he got up and ran outside. Mike and Chris raced after him.

"I had to get out of there. That woman is some voodoo princess. She's a witch, I swear. I could feel her stare in my chest."

Chris howled with laughter. "She told you straight, man. You gotta stop eating now, it's the only way."

"I don't know. I'll try it, but I feel sick," John said, resting his hands on his knees.

"I am telling y'all, Madame don't lie; you better watch yourself, Big John," Mike said.

"Okay Mike, but let's get back to the lair and watch a funny movie, maybe order a pizza or something. I think John needs to take his mind off this whole spook-show," Chris said.

"Okay, fine with me," Mike agreed.

They walked the long way home through Santa Monica, down Main Street, along Palisades Park to the winding road into the canyon, finally reaching Mike's California bungalow and their cellar hideaway at around eight o'clock.

Mike's mom immediately came down and wanted to know if they had eaten. Mike told her they had just ordered some pizza from a delivery service.

When the three enormous deep-dish pizzas from Buster's Chicago Pies arrived, loaded with extra pepperoni, hamburger, and triple cheese, John ate fast like he always did, but something inside him felt like it might be his last meal—like Madame was right there, watching him with those strange eyes. *Eat half your appetite always,* she had said. Her commanding voice was stuck in his head, all he could think about. The spicy pepperoni tasted so good on his tongue, but now he was afraid of it all. Afraid he might be alone forever. Afraid of the Madame.

5

Saturday night came around and John hadn't stopped eating one bit. In fact, just the thought of giving up food had prompted him to double up on his favorites. He went to the Vons grocery store around the corner and bought everything he could think of: bacon, a dozen eggs, four different logs of Cracker Barrel cheese, heavy whipping cream and some blueberries to go with it, a pint of Neapolitan ice cream, a dozen chocolate glazed Krispy Kreme donuts, a six-pack of Country Time lemonade in cans—his favorite—Jif peanut butter, a loaf of Wonder Bread, and some strawberry jelly also. The whole time he was shopping, he could feel Madame's eyes blazing into him, each selection a sin against her—a little lie he was telling. He could barely stand the torture, but he did it anyway.

He was going to have a big fat feast upstairs in his room while watching all his favorite movies. A real last supper. First up was *Harry and the Hendersons*, which he loved because it was set in the north woods of Seattle and was about bigfoot. Six donuts and two Country Times in, he was onto *Fletch* with Chevy Chase, a love story to the city he cherished most, Los Angeles. Around 9 p.m. he was needing some protein, so he made a four-egg and cheese omelet with half a pack of bacon. At that point, he felt Madame all around him, her blue robes curling around the four corners of his room, carrying the smell of that cursed sandalwood. By 1:30 a.m., he was finishing up Hitchcock's *Rear Window* when he fell asleep with his fourth Country Time lemonade in his hand, his shirt lifted up to expose his pale Irish belly.

Sunday, he woke up early to the LA sun and patted his belly six times with each hand, a morning ritual. The food hangover—something only real eaters like himself knew— was awful. He stared himself down in the mirror and said, "It's time, I gotta put on my best elastic shorts and get cracking on this weight thing."

His tummy kept pulling him downstairs for another omelet, but he decided his life was going to be different from that day forward. He wanted to be with Maggie, and so he kissed his old fat life goodbye. Madame had said he needed to draw what he wanted, and only eat half his appetite. Thoughts about food started to fire into his mind. He quickly pushed them away and started thinking about what he was going to draw—washboard abs. The image of himself with bulging muscles at the pool with Maggie in a tiger-striped two-piece rushed into his imagination. Every overweight man feared the bathing suit. He had always dreamed of strutting around the Montana Avenue public pool, where all the high school girls sunbathed, with a handsome cut body, looking like a stud.

As much as he loved food, the memories of it all ran

together. Once he finished eating, the pleasure vanished. He told himself he would eat his favorite snacks again one day, just not today. He would feast on Double Stuff Oreos and Girl Scout Cookies (his favorite). He would lose the weight and then have a sleeve or two of Samoas (his favorite Girl Scout Cookie). He could do that. No one would be watching him. Maggie wouldn't be waiting to see if he was eating badly again, nor would the Madame. Or would she be? Could this spell last forever?

His dad had some heavy drawing paper down in the basement, so John hurried to get it and brought it upstairs. He put on the Grateful Dead, his favorite improvisational jam band from San Francisco, and immediately began to draw his body with all his old passion for art. "Sugar Magnolia" blared through the speakers of his blue Bluetooth beach stereo. The improvisational jam band sent his mind to mysterious places.

John loved music even more than food. He liked jazz, too —any music that traveled. John Coltrane, Miles Davis, Thelonious Monk, Mingus; those were his favorites. Drawing as realistically as he could and feeling the music, he sketched every curve of the muscles around his abdomen. He drew eight wide abdominal muscles and a ripped chest too, plus the comic book superhero Thor's biceps and broad shoulders, like a swimmer. Meanwhile, the song "Cassidy" played through the speakers. That song had always rung true for him because it had a wolf in it and John had always liked canines, starting with his pug Rocky. On and on he drew, all the details of the pool and his body—short swim trunks like the French wore that showed off his new cyclist legs—beside him emerged Maggie's beautiful face.

Drawing the body of his dreams was exhilarating. On some level, he felt like the act of drawing alone was manifesting his new figure, but he knew it wasn't. How could it? Such fantasy had no basis in reality—the Madame had spent too much time around that silly ball of hers.

The finished drawing was a masterpiece of self-love. He decided it needed some color, so he got some markers and colored in every square inch of the page. Hours later, the design was complete. Standing back, he studied it in awe.

He removed his favorite Grateful Dead American Beauty poster from where it hung above his bed and tacked the drawing in its place. Then he went downstairs to eat.

Lunchtime had arrived, and food was sizzling in his mind. He took the smallest plate out of the cupboard and ate three raw baby carrots and one twirl of turkey from a big plastic circular snack platter his mom had in the fridge. That was his first time eating a raw carrot and he wanted to spit it out. When he finished eating, he was even hungrier than before, but instead of returning to the fridge, he decided to go for a walk to clear his mind.

6

T hat night, while lying in bed, Big John felt the emptiest feeling he had ever felt in his life. All these emotions came over him and his hands vibrated with that same warm energy they always had late at night. Only this time, he could no longer eat to make it go away. When he dozed off around 4 a.m., he dreamed about a sausage the size of a high rise that was attacking Los Angeles. Waking in a stupor, he stumbled into the bathroom and squinted two sleepy brown eyes at the mirror. Jumping back in alarm at the face that stared back at him, he was gripped by fear. He owned the face alright, but it was so different. It was *chiseled* and *macho*. He looked ten years older. Dumbstruck, his eyes traced his whole body, where chiseled muscle exploded from his chest to his ankles. Then he ran his hands along his abdominal muscles in a state of disbelief.

After taking a few selfies and sending them to Mike and Chris, he showered, smiling the whole time while singing the Grateful Dead's "Morning Dew." After getting out, he realized he no longer had any clothes that would fit him. He would have to go shopping. Throwing on what had been his tightest old clothes that he had bought right after fat camp, he pulled his belt to the last hole and raced downstairs and out the door, unseen, past his parents who were having breakfast. The smell of the cooking bacon grease and grand biscuits didn't faze him. Besides, he had no clue how he would begin to explain his new figure to his parents, or if they would even recognize him.

John sort of danced while he walked all the way to J. Crew on the Santa Monica Third Street Promenade, where he had agreed to meet Mike and Chris. They were desperate to see his new figure, thinking he had used a filter to somehow doctor the photos.

"Dude, who are you and what did you do with my friend?" Mike asked John as he approached. Flabbergasted, he grabbed John's bicep to see if it was real.

"It's me, guys. That gypsy juju actually worked! I drew myself looking like this, and I woke up today looking like an action figure. I can't explain it."

"What about Maggie? She won't even recognize you now. You can't see her until Spring Break is over. It would take you months to get in this kind of shape."

"*Oh, damn guys*, you're right. I didn't even think of that. What I am going to do?"

"I don't know, screw it," Mike said.

The boys went inside J. Crew and John tried on all the skinny jeans and thin person clothes he never could have dreamed of wearing before. He bought them all with his parent's credit card he had for clothing expenses. After leaving J. Crew, cute girls and even grown women were checking John out everywhere the group went along the promenade. A knock-out with flame-red hair and equally red lipstick asked him for his number at the Coffee Bean. He gave it to her even though she was probably five years older than him.

John got home at dusk. His mom had texted him throughout the day to check on him, and he told her he was at Mike's. Although it made no sense—he would have to see his parents eventually—John still tried sneaking in through the garage door and up the back stairwell. That's when his mom, Susan, immediately picked up a broom and tried to attack him.

"*Stop...wait...it's me, Mom!* It's Big John!"

Quickly, he moved into the light, and she recognized his face right away.

"Oh honey, you have changed. It is you! *What happened?*" She stroked a hand along his face.

"I don't know, I just woke up and I was thin like this," he said, shrugging.

"What? Well, we've got to take you to the doctor. Come, let's show your father now."

John followed his mother into the living room, where his dad, Henry, a bald man in his late fifties, was reading the newspaper. He didn't look up.

"Henry, look at John."

"Yeah, yeah, he looks great," he said, continuing to read.

"*No!* Henry, *look* at your son. He is thin! He has changed *overnight.*"

Henry lowered the newspaper and looked at his son over his tortoiseshell reading glasses.

"You look good, John! What you been doing, working out?" he said, vaguely squinting to take in his son's appearance.

"I just went to the gym a lot last week, pop, that's all."

"Good, keep it up. Maybe you can play high school ball now and get a scholarship to USC, so I don't have to pay for it." He went back to his paper.

"Henry, your son has *really changed* overnight! Now, I think we should take him to some kind of specialist."

"No Mom, I don't want to go!"

"Oh hell, leave the boy alone," Henry said, glancing up over his paper. "Can't you see he just had a little growth spurt? He's trying to make it in high school. That is the hardest place in the world to be. It's a battleground, I tell you."

"See Mom, it's fine. Thanks, Dad. I gotta go upstairs now. I am so tired."

"Okay, but promise me you won't lift any more weight—you are too fit, John."

"I promise. Love you."

At that moment, John's beloved dog, Rocky, a pug with a waistline a tad too thick, wagged over to John with his tongue hanging hopelessly out of his mouth. John showered the little dog he loved so dearly with affection. After a few minutes of petting Rocky, John excused himself and went upstairs to sleep. The next day, he had big plans to go walking along Montana Avenue and be seen by some ladies.

7

J ohn strolled down Montana Avenue, wearing a pair of faded stone-washed blue jeans and a white V-neck T-shirt that glued to his new muscles on the electric day of sunshine under a perfect blue sky.

He desperately wanted to see Maggie May and show off his new body, but he knew it would have to wait until spring break was over. Mike and Chris were right about that.

As he cruised past the hip funky boutiques lining the street, he noticed a red Ferrari up ahead. A well-groomed Latin man got out, wearing a white linen oxford with a baby blue shirt beneath. As he approached John, he stopped in front of him, extending his grand, tan hand.

"I am Federico, nice to meet you."

"John," John said, shaking the man's hand.

"Man, you've really got the look, my friend. What agency are you with?" Federico put his hands on his hips. John noticed the gold he was wearing.

"No agency."

"Really? Well, it's our lucky day. Take my card. I want to represent you. I am the biggest independent agent for models and actors in LA."

"Wow, thanks," John said, taking the card and studying it.

"We are having a big party tonight at the Kirkeby Mansion in Beverly Hills. Everyone is going to be there. You should come."

"Okay, neat. I will be there."

"Give me your number and I will text you the address."

"All right, thanks boss."

As Federico walked away, John stood there baffled in amazement. During his fat days, no one ever invited him and The Zoo Crew to parties. Come to think of it, no one invited them anywhere. Now he was going to a party at the Kirkeby Mansion in Beverly Hills with connected people. Dreams of fame flashed through his mind. Doing a happy dance, he glided down the street. He wrote Federico to put Mike and Chris on the guest list.

That night, Mike, Chris, and John pulled up in a taxi to the sprawling mansion and stepped out dressed head to toe in their best garments.

As they approached the mansion, their jaws slacked open in disbelief and time seemed to stop for a moment. Up ahead, a herd of lingerie models walked through the mahogany front door. The three chuckled and pointed.

Inside, they were greeted by more opulence than they had ever witnessed in their short lives. Famous actors and musicians and models mingled in the stew of the cocktail party.

The three went over to the hors d'oeuvres table after

John ordered them three whiskey sours from the open bar—his cleft chin passed for his ID.

After handing his buddies the drinks, John started piling sliders, deviled eggs, and caviar on his plate. The plate stacked high with food by the time he reached the end of the table, he was about to gobble it all up, but Madame's voice seared into his brain. He could see himself getting fat again in an instant, so he dumped the plate in the trash and got a new one, tossing on some carrots and pickles along with a ham twirl, and ate it all very slowly, savoring every morsel.

A drop-dead gorgeous blonde in a tight black sequin cocktail dress approached him and started flirting.

"What's your name? I'm Mercedes." She took a baby carrot off his plate and sucked on it slowly.

"John," he said politely and smiled. She ate the carrot.

"You know, I don't usually come to these things."

"Me neither," John said.

"Who do you work for?"

"Well, I just signed with Federico."

"Oh, he's *so* great, you'll *adore* him. He'll *do anything* for you." She turned and placed her hands on the table, arching her back and looking up into his eyes with a sexy gaze. "I once had this job for Victoria's Secret and he got me five figures for it. No joke."

"Really? Yeah, you do look familiar," John said and turned his head away, amazed by the dull conversation. At that moment, Mercedes slid her hand down his leg, touching his crotch. He almost got an erection in front of everyone, but started thinking about fire alarms and stopped that event from occurring.

Right at that moment, across the room, his eye caught a

stunning Asian woman. She had long natural wavy black hair and wasn't wearing much make-up, but she had the most radiant natural beauty ever. Her dressed-down T-shirt and white jeans appealed to John, awash in the sea of jackets and cocktail dresses.

John pried his body from Mercedes's spell and walked over to the dazzling woman. When he got to her, by accident, he slipped and fell. The Asian girl immediately rushed over to help him, which impressed him even more.

"Oh, I am so sorry, are you okay?"

"Yeah, I guess so," John said, looking up into her eyes. He was lost in the dark recesses of her soul. "How are you?"

"I am fine. My name's Angela."

"Nice to meet you, I'm John. People call me Big John though, usually. What are you doing here?"

"I am a singer. Federico is my agent. I am just getting started. Had my first solo gig at Whiskey a Go Go last weekend."

"Oh, sweet! I love music. Hey, you want me to grab you a drink?" John asked.

At that moment, a man with black slicked-back hair and a grey beard, wearing a midnight suit approached. It was Angela's manager, Tom Mason.

"Angela, who is this lad you are talking with?" Tom asked.

"This is John, he's a...?"

"A model," John said, extending his hand.

"Oh great, Tom Mason, nice to meet you." Tom looked unimpressed by John.

"Angela, let's make the rounds, there's some people I want to introduce you to."

"Okay sure. Bye John, it was so nice to meet you."

Angela and Tom vanished into the swirl of wealthy suits and designer dresses in the living room. Mike and Chris walked over.

"Did you see Bradley Cooper is here!?" Mike said.

"Yeah and we just saw Margot Robbie walk by while we were on our way to the bathroom. This is so rad," Chris said.

"Really? Wow, some blonde model grabbed my pecker. It was incredible," John bragged, even though the event had been less than exciting to him.

"Really, no way!"

"Yeah, this 'being fit' thing has its perks," John said and laughed.

At that moment, someone got thrown in the pool outside and the crowd of Italian designer jackets followed the racket out through the opened French doors to see what all the commotion was about. Many people began jumping in the pool fully dressed as well.

The crew mingled for a while, but when the clock struck ten, they knew they had to get back to Mike's basement before his mom found out they were missing.

That night, the trio stayed up until the sun rose, talking about the party and all the people they'd seen. It was a brave new world, one of flash and fame. One of opulence. One that was completely unknown to them. They all had dreams now, even Mike and Chris, of being famous one day and rolling in such circles like it was no big deal.

8

E arly the next morning, John said goodbye to his buddies and went home. Around noon, he got a call from Federico for his first modeling gig, a Ralph Lauren shoot on the beach in Malibu. John needed to be there that afternoon, and the gig drew $20,000. John almost dropped the phone, speechless when Federico said the amount. In a whirlwind of business frenzy, Federico emailed a contract and put John's parents in touch with a manager named Bob Floss. Susan, John's mom, still in a slight state of shock at John's new appearance, allowed the possibility of easy money to override any fears she had, which were plentiful. She printed out the contract, signed her consent, and scanned and emailed it back to Bob later that afternoon. That signature marked the beginning of John's new life as a model. And he was certain Maggie May would be very impressed; all he could think about was telling her the whole story, starting from his fateful appointment with the fortune-teller.

The Ralph Lauren shoot started with John removing his shirt and getting his body wet in the ocean while wearing a pair of khaki cargo shorts. Next, some slinky model his age from Colombia with large breasts crawled into his arms while they frolicked in the sea.

When the shoot was over, he desperately wanted to post the shot with the Latin model as his Facebook profile image right away to show off to Maggie, but he knew everyone would by shocked by his sudden appearance change.

While waiting in his trailer they had provided him to use for the day, the girl, whose name was Valentina and who turned out to be two years older than him, knocked on the trailer door. He swung it open and she pounced, pulling him to the sofa. They made out for a while before she left. The moment washed over him like he had won the lottery. A girl like that never would have given him the time of day before. He wanted more attention like that from beautiful women.

Now he wondered about Maggie May and what she would do when she saw his new appearance. He just had to give her a call. He had gotten her name and number from Chris who knew a girlfriend of hers and had it stored in his phone. John had never been brave enough to call Maggie, but he felt free of that now. Dialing her number, he waited, his heart pounding in his chest.

"Hello?" she answered.

"Hey Maggie, it's Big John."

"John, hey guy, how are you?"

"Great, I am actually on my first modeling gig in Malibu for Ralph Lauren."

"*What? Modeling? Really?* That's cool. So you are representing the plus-size thing?"

"Well, no, it's not like that. It's Ralph Lauren."

"Hey John, I gotta run, my mom needs me to take our Yorkshire to the doggie spa for her daily meditation and hypnotherapy. Thanks for calling, though," she said and hung up abruptly.

"Bye," he said, hopelessly too late, and hung up. Sitting back on the sofa, depressed, he tried dreaming of Maggie May. His hands were tingling all of a sudden, and he had Eggo waffles on the brain. He could knock out about five of those waffles with half a stick of butter right now. The bad talk with Maggie activated his appetite and lust for food. Reese's Peanut Butter Cup fantasies flooded his mind.

Wandering outside, he raced to the window of the food truck on the beach for the actors, where he ordered two double cheeseburgers, a large French fry, and a strawberry milkshake. He couldn't control himself, his hands now shaking and tingling with that same annoying warmth. Once back in his trailer, he savored every bite.

His belly poked out with that full feeling he loved so much, and he knew, tomorrow, he would be his old fat self again.

But nothing happened right away. The $20,000 was wired to his parent's bank account that evening. And his mom transferred a healthy amount to John's little personal checking account.

By the next morning, John woke up to Big John staring back at him. It was a nightmare—he scurried around his room, trying to figure out what to do. He put on his biggest elastic fat clothes and rode his bike straight to Venice to see the gypsy.

He rushed into her "seeing room," but she was with someone.

"Oh Big John, my friend, you have returned. Have a seat in my waiting room."

John was out of breath and panting. "Please tell me, how do I get skinny again? I ate too much yesterday and all the fat came back. Look at my arms, they are a giggling mess!" he said, shaking his right arm in the air.

"Can't you see I am with a client, John?"

"Yes, I see that, but you have to help me! I need help. This is terrible."

"Go wait in the lobby. I will be with you shortly."

John paced around the room, doing circles like a nervous rooster. The client, a young hippie woman in her mid-twenties, wearing blue jean shorts and a floral blouse, hopped out, and John raced in.

"Help me, Madame, please!" John said, placing his hands on the table and leaning forward. "Please make me skinny again, now. I can't go back to my old life."

"Oh, Big John," she said, leaning back in her green chair. "How did this happen? Look at you! You feasted, my dear, didn't you?"

"Yes, yes, I admit it. I couldn't help it! All this raw emotion came over me after talking to Maggie, and I had to eat to make it go away. And these damn hands, they tingle all the time!"

"Well, control your appetite again and wait for two days, and the body you desire will return."

"That's it?"

"Yes. It's that simple. The drawing you made is a magical spell on all the fat cells in your body, and it's controlled by what you eat. Eat thin, and you will be thin—eat fat, and you will be fat."

"Okay, done! Thank you, Madame," John said and paid her the $50 fee and rushed out.

At home, he spent the next two days dodging his parents, sending them texts from upstairs that he was ill with a cold. He relayed to Mike and Chris what had happened. His mom and dad had worked all the time since he was younger just trying to afford their expensive Santa Monica Canyon house. His father, an estate and will lawyer and his mom, a freelance graphic designer, did everything they could to pay the bills on the house. Modern life in West LA was expensive.

All John ate was baby carrots and some nuts he rationed for each meal, which he had hidden in a plastic freezer bag.

Two days later, he woke up with a chiseled body again. When he looked in the mirror, he felt certain he looked just like Michelangelo's statue of David. Seeing the sculpture on his family's trip to Italy two years ago, he had wondered then how many dates he would get if he looked like that. Now, he *was* David. Calling Federico, the two set a time for a lunch meeting. Being fit and modeling now left a savory taste in John's mouth the way food used to.

After dressing, John pranced outside. Since getting his new physique, he had a compulsion to be around other people. He needed to be seen. It just felt so good when women flirted with him.

Federico picked him up in a silver Lamborghini and they drove to Huckleberry on Wilshire Avenue. The café was packed with beautiful women who all ogled John while he ordered. He couldn't decide what to have—it was all so *delicious* and *off-limits*—so he ordered a half a Caesar salad.

Federico tortured him slowly as he ate his blueberry scone.
Every bite struck John right in the belly. He longed for that
full feeling again and for his belly to poke out, but only
when he was tempted by food.

They talked about John's modeling career, Federico
informing John that he had booked him for four more gigs
in the next week, all bringing handsome wages. John was
thrilled. And he was gradually forgetting about his old life
with Mike and Chris. Santa Monica High felt so distant. So
much had happened during the first week of spring break,
and there was still another week to go.

Over that next week, he went to the gigs—one for Gucci,
one for J. Crew, another for Abercrombie and Fitch, and
finally, one for a surfboard company called Raze. His
parent's bank account exploded with wealth—$83,500 from
the five gigs.

Mike and Chris kept calling and John would text that he
was on location, but he missed them and would see them
again soon.

Resisting the urge to eat was brutal on most days. His
diet, now consisting mainly of salads, pickles, small amounts
of fruit and baby carrots, some ham and turkey twirls off the
snack platter—all in small portions—took enormous
willpower to maintain. At the same time, after that first short
week of modeling, something magical had already started to
churn inside him. The combination of eating little to no food
and all the adoration from everyone around him sent John
longing for another world, one where people were valued
for their inner essence and not how they looked. That night
he lay in bed, asking himself what it all meant. Why was he

here on earth? If it wasn't to be adored or to eat, then what was it all about?

He still was desperately in love with Maggie May and wondered what she thought about such things. He decided to ask her tomorrow on their first day back from Spring Break. He could hardly sleep fantasizing about seeing her again, what she would be wearing, what it would be like and what they would say. He wanted to bare his new soul to her.

9

The day Big John returned to school, as he strutted down the halls, the attractive girls' mouths dropped to the floor in amazement. And when he glanced at them, they blushed. No one even recognized him as Big John, they thought he was a new kid. And then there was Maggie May. He made his way to her locker like a bobcat on a mission. She looked up in sheer bafflement at his new face and figure.

"*John?* Is that you?"

"Yeah, it's me. I got fit quickly. How was your spring break, love?"

"It was ... uh ... good ... uh, *what happened* to you?" she said, her eyes the size of golf balls.

"I just hit the gym really hard over the break. I am a model now. Anyway, want to go out sometime?" He said it so confidently, it surprised even him.

"Sure! I would love to!" She was blushing with a cherry red face. "Some girlfriends and I are having some friends over at my house today, it's a pool party. I would love it if you could come." She started sucking on the tip of her pen.

"Okay, I am there."

"Here, give me your hand," she said, taking the pen from her mouth and picking his right hand up. A surge of energy jolted through his palm, which kind of felt uncomfortable as she wrote her address on it.

"Come by about three o'clock."

"Okay, I'll be there."

"I'll be waiting." She waved as she walked away.

John was flying high on the inside. A knock-out had just invited him to a pool party at her house. Superman would finally conquer his kryptonite—the swimming pool.

Soon, Mike and Chris walked up.

"Hey stranger," Mike said.

"Where have you been hiding, buddy?" Chris asked.

"I've been so busy on these modeling gigs, guys. So sorry I didn't call. There is so much I want to tell you."

"Was that Maggie you were talking to, you bad ass?" Mike asked.

"Oh yeah, I'm going to her house today," he said, holding up his palm to reveal the address.

"No way, sweet!" Chris said. "Hey, can we tag along?"

"Oh yeah, sure. Maybe—let me ask. I'll text you, I gotta go to class now. Let's talk later."

"All right boss," Mike said; then, turning to Chris, "He's a legend."

10

That afternoon, at the pool, Big John walked toward Maggie's blue and white lounge chair, showing off his sculpted body in all its glorious fashion. He had removed his shirt as soon as he walked out onto the patio. Maggie's house was an enormous mansion in the canyon around the corner from Mike's house. All the coolest and hottest girls were there, laying out, bronzing their thin bodies under the hot California sun.

Maggie leaned up to make room for John, patting the foot of her lounge. John sat.

"So, John, tell us, what is your secret? I mean, you are like so hot now," said Vanessa, one of Maggie's best friends, peering at him over the top of her white cat eye sunglasses.

"I don't know, I just did a thousand of those ab rolls every day and stopped eating so much."

"Well, it worked babe," Vanessa said. "You are fabulous now, boy."

"You're a stud now," Maggie said, rubbing his leg with her freshly red painted toes.

"You're one of us," said Pierce, Vanessa's boyfriend. Cut like an ox, he played quarterback for the school's football team. "Have a cold one on me, bro." He handed John an ice-cold beer. John opened it and took his first sip.

"Thanks," John said.

A buzz came through on John's cell. It was Chris texting to see if he and Mike could come over.

"Hey, could my buddies Chris and Mike stop by?" John asked Maggie.

Maggie looked stunned, "You're not referring to that *Zoo Crew*, are you?"

"Yeah, I just thought they could come hang also. They are my best friends."

"Hey bud, you gotta ditch those two critters you hang with. Those guys are whack. You're one of us." Pierce took out a vape and offered it to John who passed.

John couldn't believe how shallow and exclusive these people were acting.

"Maggie tells us you're some kind of big shot model now?" Mack asked.

"Yeah, I guess so."

"Hey, did you meet Tom Ford?" asked Lexy, a short brunette with a nose like Tinkerbell. "Maggie said you work for Gucci?"

"No, not yet. Chris and Mike and I went to some party in Beverly Hills and saw all kinds of famous people there."

"You took those two babies to a famous person party?" Maggie said in disbelief, her mouth hanging opened.

"Yeah, of course."

"So, tell us, who all did you see?" Pierce asked.

"Well I didn't recognize anyone, but Mike and Chris saw Bradley Cooper and Margot Robbie."

"Oh, Bradley is such a hottie," Lexy said.

"I know, right," Maggie said.

After a while, everyone left except John and Maggie. She slid over to him and whispered in his ear. He smiled, but he was so annoyed by the conversation, he was a little turned off by her now. Still, the two started kissing. He decided to reveal to her what had happened with the gypsy.

"Hey Maggie—you know, I want to tell you, it was really this fortune-teller gypsy who cured me of being fat. That is why I look this way now."

"What?" she said in disbelief. "Come here," she said, ignoring him and pulling him closer.

"No—I mean, didn't you hear what I said?"

"I heard you. That's sexy."

He smiled, thinking she might have gotten it. "Hey, what do you want in life?" John asked.

"Right now, I want you, you big stud."

They kissed again. He pulled away, "But tell me, what do you dream about?"

"Stuff, of course. A Rolls-Royce. A house in the hills."

"No, I mean what do you want spiritually? I have been thinking about that lately a lot with this weight loss and all."

"Oh, you are so deep—that's sexy, too." She moved her hand along his body.

He smiled, "No, I'm serious babe. What do you want out of life?"

"You are ruining the moment, John. I don't know. I just want to have fun. Leave me alone." She got up, wrapped a beach towel around her waist, and said, "Let me know when you decide what you want, John. I'm here when you're ready." Then she walked briskly toward the pool house.

John couldn't believe this was the girl he had waited so many years for. He had lustily dreamed about this moment since the fifth grade and finally it had arrived, in all its misery and sadness. Angela popped into his mind—the beautiful Asian soul singer he had met on Bel Air Road that night. Now, he wanted to tell *her* about Madame Bernadette and the cure, and ask her these questions about life—and he had a feeling that *she* would have *real answers*. John exited through the back gate and hustled home.

11

On the way home, he cruised up to Montana Avenue for a nitro cold brew coffee. He drank little coffee now, and always black. He was terrified his belly would come back with the slightest intake of dairy. While walking, he saw a flier advertising Angela Omni acoustic live at the Whiskey a Go Go that Saturday at 8 p.m. He took a photo of the flier and raced home.

John missed his buddies, Mike and Chris. Things had slowed down. He could only model on the weekends due to school, which greatly limited what gigs he could be hired for. He called his friends and they agreed to rendezvous at Mike's lair that night.

John shared with them what had happened with Maggie, and they were ashamed to learn how they were perceived by that set. John couldn't stand their reaction, so he changed the subject to why humanity was on earth and what it all means. Mike had some refreshing comments that "life is a stratosphere of desire"; Chris said, "We should all just go to mass every week."

Chris was from a very old Catholic family, and John expected more from him. John respected Chris's faith and he even had compassion for him because to not respect a person's faith was bigotry. But, in the emptiness of John's belly, something was calling out—and it wasn't for food anymore, nor for Maggie or the respect of his peers. It was for love and faith. Like descending into the ocean, he grew deeper with every passing minute. The three laughed together, but no real answers about life emerged. John felt better to have spent time with them nonetheless, although he experienced a sad sense of distance forming between them as he walked out into the crisp awakened night. He sensed no one, not even his closest friends, knew what he was talking about—at least, no one his age. To stop his mind from constantly churning over his questions about life, he decided to start exercising.

And so, he began to run, relentlessly, on the trails up in Topanga near Malibu. One night, he wandered off the beaten dusty trail and saw an enormous round rock; he decided to climb the boulder to get a better view of the valley below. Standing on top of it, he stared into the beautiful, mesmerizing night sky, speckled with stars, and he gave thanks for being alive.

When he spun around, on a stump to the left, he saw an oversized buzzard—a symbol of death. It was true that the John of his old fat life had died, and now, his new persona as a model—as someone the Maggie Mays of the world would invite in—was dying. He now believed many models were probably genuine people because they were adored so much by people attending to their container and not their content, which caused them to value depth. The other day a model had offered to drive him home thirty minutes out of his way and he was the kindest person he had ever spoken to. A spark shone in his eye also. While it was true that the beauty business was making him see the shallowness of the things he coveted, he couldn't handle all the attention to his appearance. The buzzard squawked loudly and flew off toward the sea.

At school, life buzzed on. He tried to enjoy how everyone adored his appearance, but secretly he sulked when he was alone. He ate lunch with Mike and Chris every day, and the crew had broadly managed to maintain the lives they'd had before John's transformation. He simply didn't talk with them—or anyone—about his feelings around life and God.

12

Saturday night, John was in the front row for Angela Omni's performance. At the all-ages nightclub Whiskey a Go Go, Angela lived up to her name—her angelic voice and music radiated soul.

The first song she sang was a bluesy rendition of "Baby, Please Don't Go" by Muddy Waters, another one of John's favorite musicians. And the second song moved like a train. John danced the soles on his shoes bare that night. Angela and he made eye contact a few times; each time, her face turned pink and she flashed him a wicked smile.

After the show, he waited out back where the bands exited, leaning against the wall. As she walked out with her guitar slung over her shoulder, he stopped her.

"Hey girl!"

"Oh—hey ... John, right? From the party at the Kirkeby Mansion?"

"Yeah, that's me all right. I loved hearing you sing

tonight. Let me tell you, what you just did up there, oh my, you're amazing."

She smiled and looked down and back up at him. "Aww, thanks for saying that—and for coming. It means a lot to me. My career is just getting started."

"Well you're advanced, believe me. I know music. There are two things I know: food and music. And you're great."

"Aww, you're so sweet. Thanks, let's get together sometime."

"Well, how about now?" John said, smiling as wide as The Golden Gate Bridge.

"Like ... right now?"

"Yeah, why not?"

"Okay, let me put my guitar in the car."

"Okay, awesome." He followed her over to her new blue Prius. "Cool wheels, girl. I still don't have my license. One year to go. It's lame, I know."

"Thanks, I paid for it myself by playing gigs."

"Really? That's amazing. But I have to ask, how old are you?"

"Seventeen. I know, everyone tells me I look twenty-one. I guess when you're a teenager, it's a compliment to be mistaken as older, but when you are an older lady, you would rather be mistaken as younger."

"Funny how people change that way, with age I mean."

"I know, right? It really is so stupid if you think about it. When I'm sixty-one, I want people to think I am an old dame. I am going to wear big funky designer jewelry and have a collection of cats. Of course, I want to be fit and look good, but I don't care if someone thinks I'm forty. Who even cares about it?"

"Not me. I am with you," John said, smiling.

The two walked along Sunset and stopped in an organic yogurt joint. They sat across from each other, laughing and eating.

"So, tell me about you? What makes you tick?" she asked him.

"Everything. These days, I want to find the meaning to life. I want to know why I am here. What's my soul's place?"

"Sounds ambitious, but I hear you. Music gives my life meaning and depth. It touches my soul. That's why I sing, you know," she said, and smiled while spooning some more vanilla yogurt.

"Music feels that way to me also. I have listened to music since I was a small boy. I used to take out my dad's old vinyl records and play them one after another. I still know them all by heart. But I never really could play an instrument. I tried guitar, but my hands would always tingle so badly when I strummed that I had to quit. I prefer to listen anyway."

"Your hands tingled? That's funny."

"Yeah I know, tell me about it."

"Well, there is nothing like the way vinyl sounds." She paused. "So, what's with the modeling thing? You don't seem like the type, really."

"It's just a way to make money. I am over it already and I just started," he said, laughing.

After finishing their yogurts, he walked her back to her car, where they kissed for a long time. She leaned up on her tiptoes, which he knew was a good sign. He felt a warm tingling feeling all over his whole body and his hands were on fire in a good way.

"How about that for feeling alive?" she posed the question to him.

"Oh yeah, that's good!" he said.

The next evening, Angela had a gig in Malibu, so John slept in and then spent the afternoon listening to her YouTube videos. He was already in love with her—that, he could feel in his bones. He wanted to marry her, he thought.

After eating a beggar's meal for supper of more baby carrots and one ham twirl, he raced out into the night. Last night's yogurt was a close call for John. Madame was in that shop watching him, he could feel her there. He had ordered the low-fat Greek flavor and when Angela asked him why, he blamed it on the modeling career.

Mike and Chris called, but John had started feeling uneasy around them, like they didn't understand him. He hated to leave them, but he was a soul-searcher now. Questions about life penetrated him, and buddies or not, they didn't care or want to know the answers.

13

T oday, he was determined to return to Topanga and find that damn buzzard again. He rode his bike toward Malibu, visiting his usual spots. The buzzard was nowhere to be found, even at the rock where he had first encountered it. He decided to break and climb the rock again.

"Hello," he yelled from the top of the rock.

He waited for a response, but heard nothing, and then he walked down the trail further into the night. The sky swirled with a beautiful indigo to it.

After about one third of a mile, he saw the bird again. It squawked loudly and then flew straight toward him. Landing five feet away, it transformed into the most exquisite woman he had ever set eyes on. Dressed head to toe in robes that matched the sky, they eerily reminded him of the gypsy, Madame Bernadette. He knew it was her, but why the new appearance? In her right arm, she gripped a long, wooden staff with a golden orb shining like a firefly in the night. The light emanating from it exuded warmth.

"Madame? Is that you?"

"Yes, John. I am here to help you."

"But why do you care about helping me?"

"You don't know this, but I know you. Your grandmother helped me when I was a young girl, orphaned by my mother. She found a family for me to live with, and they helped me to become the woman I am now."

"Really? Wow. But you don't look the same. You are so much more beautiful than your other look."

"We only see what we want to see. I am the same there as I am here. You see a plain French woman and don't see behind the veil. Hiding inside her heart is a brilliant spiritual essence. Always learn to look beyond the pale."

"I think I understand. I am getting tired of people worshiping the way I look. But I don't want to go back to being fat again, either."

"I know. The world we live in is a world of appearances. Because you have transcended food now by constantly measuring what you eat, you have freed yourself from the constant craving and set out on an inward journey. You can return to eating the foods you enjoy now without the curse of your old weight—but continue to eat wisely. Bad foods will slowly and steadily make you fat again, just as they do to everyone. The United States is suffering from an obesity epidemic pushed by the processed food industry. They don't want you to be fit."

"Okay, I understand." John's hands began to feel very strange. He looked down and saw them glowing with an aural light.

"Wow, what's this?" he said, holding his hands out in front of him in disbelief.

"Use them wisely, John. You were born to be a healer one day."

"*What? A what?*"

"Use your intuition and see what happens. Go forward now."

"Okay, but I want you to teach me how to turn into a bird like you, so I can fly into the wind."

"Always look for the white wolf. He is your guide now, not a bird. Maybe that's why you like the Grateful Dead song 'Cassidy.'" And then she turned into a stark white owl and darted off into the night.

John's hands stopped glowing, but he felt energy running through them.

He returned to his house and lay in bed, staring at the ceiling. Studying his hands carefully, he thought about what the gypsy had told him—that he would be a healer one day. Now, he had to test it out. His dog, Rocky, was always hobbling around and he had these lumpy benign tumors all over his stomach. It pained John's heart every time the little dude walked by. Scheduled for surgery in a few days, John saw no downside to trying to do something.

It was 3 a.m., but John decided to sneak downstairs and work on Rocky. John found the dog lying in his brown dog bed in the kitchen, snoring away. Startled by John's footsteps, Rocky woke up, yawned, and stretched his legs. John kneeled down beside his old friend and began gently petting Rocky's stomach. Next, he held one of his hands over one of the lumps, focusing with all of his intent on it disappearing. As he did so, he could feel energy flowing through his hand. He held his place there for a minute or two, during which time he could sense the lump gradually diminishing. A miracle no less; John simply couldn't believe it. He proceeded to work on all of Rocky's lumps with the same amazing results.

The next day, John dialed Angela, and she agreed to come pick him up in forty-five minutes. While John waited downstairs in the living room with his father, Henry complained of another series of cluster headaches. Migraines had plagued the man his whole life, since he was a small child. John went over and placed his hand on his father's forehead.

"Let me see if you have a fever, Dad," John said.

"No fever, I get these all the time. You know that."

John held his palm there with the intention that the pain go away. After a minute, his dad said, "Wow I think the pain is gone, John. My goodness. Must have been that Tylenol I took. Just kicked in, I guess."

"Yeah, I bet you're right," John agreed.

John walked outside where he sat on the porch of his modest two-story California Spanish house, waiting for Angela. He imagined what he might do with his new gift. Could he heal everyone? That was too hard to even think about—unimaginable. No, he would start with one person and go from there.

The cerulean blue Prius coasted silently toward John, and as he stepped through the passenger door, he thought Angela looked so *California* in her designer stonewashed jeans, white T-shirt, Birkenstocks, and a straw sun hat—a subtle amount of makeup, not nearly as much as Maggie May.

And she had the Grateful Dead's "Scarlet Begonias" playing.

"Nice song."

Thanks. I love the Dead."

"No way! Me too!"

"No way! Cool. Are we going to my place today?"

"That's the plan. You look awesome, by the way."

"Thanks."

Angela lived near the beach in Malibu. The pair drove along the dazzling rugged coastline up Pacific Highway 1 for about twenty minutes before they finally turned left into a neighborhood of mostly high-end renovated mobile homes that had been turned into multimillion-dollar residences. Her father, Preecha Omni, had a little square beige-colored hideaway nestled in a cove of eucalyptus trees. Angela parked and they hustled inside. Her yellow golden retriever, Buster, lay on the porch, giving them no mind as they approached.

Angela's father wasn't home, so she took John around back to her room, which was a renovated old 1960s airstream RV trailer Preecha had placed for her in the backyard. The thick smell of eucalyptus embossed the air.

"Wow, this is so great, babe!"

"Yeah, isn't it amazing? Dad did this for me so I could practice my guitar at night without keeping him up. How cool is my dad?" she said, smiling.

"Cool dad indeed. Where's your mom?"

"She died when I was five, in a car crash."

"Oh, I am so sorry to hear that."

"Don't be—it was a long time ago. Dad and I have had a

great life. I do miss her, though, all the time. I write songs
about her. Want to hear one?"

"Sure."

They entered the trailer and sat on a brown sofa with
white polka dots in the living room. She picked up her guitar
and started to strum it and sing gently with her angelic voice.

Your soul was wild and free

Swimming in the vast sea with me

We were young and beautiful

Time's a great mystery

No time to worry now

You're gone but I still feel you running free

In the wind and through the clouds

Sometimes you come and speak to me

"That's really beautiful, babe."

"Thanks. I write a lot about the ocean, water, and nature.
Those are my elements. It's where I feel free," she said as she
leaned the guitar up against the wall. "So, what have you
been up to?"

"Well, if I tell you, you might not believe me. But I am
going to tell you anyway. I just have to tell someone or I
swear I might burst. If you are the kind of person I think you
are, then you will be fascinated. Last night, I saw this mysterious buzzard in Topanga. I followed it and it magically
turned into a beautiful woman who blessed my hands,
which started glowing, and she told me I would be a healer
one day."

Angela looked surprised.

"You're serious!" she said, her jaw dropping.

"Yes, indeed. I didn't believe it either, but I held my hand
over my dog Rocky's tumors last night and they just disap-

peared in an instant. Then again, this morning, I made my dad's migraine go away. It swear it's a miracle!"

"Well, maybe you can heal me also."

"Maybe—what's wrong?"

"I am 80 percent deaf in my left ear. I had a bad ear infection when I was a child and my hearing never returned. It really interferes with my music sometimes."

"I don't know if I can help, but it's worth a try."

"Thanks," she said, leaning forward toward him. He turned to face her, placing his hand on her left ear. Within a minute of holding it there, he felt her ear grow very warm and tingle. Then he let go.

"Did it work?"

"I think so! Wow, it feels different. I don't know, speak into my left ear for me."

"Hello, lovely."

"I can hear you! I can hear! This is *so amazing*! Oh my God! You are some kind of miracle worker now, John."

"I wouldn't say that. I don't feel like one, anyway. It's just me, John. The same guy who kissed you the other night. I think it's the energy in my hands, I am like some kind of super conductor and the energy just flows through my hands into the body, removing the blockage. Everything is energy at some level. All matter is energy. That's how I think of it anyway."

"I see what you mean. Well, I have another problem that you can fix?"

"What's that?"

"I need a kiss right now to heal my need for your love."

John leaned in and embraced her.

Suddenly, they heard a rapping on the Airstream door.

The two scrambled away from each other. Standing up, Angela fixed her clothes and opened the door.

"Hey Pa, I want you to meet my new boyfriend, John."

John hopped up and extended his hand to shake Preecha's.

"*Sewadee krap*, John. That's how we say hello in Thailand."

"*Sewadee krap*," John said back.

"Thank you. Will you be staying for dinner tonight? It's Thai food, and I am cooking."

"Sure, I'd love to."

Angela and John followed Preecha through the back door of the main house, where they hung around the white marbled island while he prepared and cooked the food. The smell of freshly ground red chili and green curry wafted into the air.

"Guess what, dad? I have something to tell you."

"What is it, angel?"

"John cured my ear tonight with his hands. He has some kind of gift."

"Really? Wow my child, that is super special."

"Yeah, I know. Remember how you used to tell me about that Buddhist monk from your village in Thailand who could heal people with his hands?"

"Yes—Chayan. I remember the man well. He cured everyone and everything."

"Well, John is like that, father."

John smiled uncomfortably, not sure how his new gift would be received.

"Is that so? All right, my friend, from now on, you will

work on me every time I get sick, and in return, I will make you all the Thai food your heart desires."

"You got it. I want to tell you, Angela—I have a passion for Thai food."

"Well, you will love Pa's food then. He is the best Thai cook."

"What are we having tonight?" John said, watching Preecha cut up the onions and vegetables like a master chef.

"It's my own creation. I make up my own menu each night. I experiment by placing certain ingredients together. It's usually a little different every time, and some amazing food comes from my experimentations." He dipped a spoon into a bowl and held it up to John, saying, "Taste this."

"That's delicious."

John no longer lusted after food. He was over that. All the crap food he had lived on for so long was dead to him. Sub-existing on carrots for weeks had changed his palate. Now, he was a sophisticated eater. He liked flavors instead of fat, and he knew there was more to cuisine than just salty and sweet. The mainstream garbage he had for so long eaten indiscriminately really only catered to those two flavors— salty and sweet—and they usually overdid both.

"You know, I used to be really fat, until recently," John said.

"Really, but you're so fit now!" Angela said.

"Yeah—people have called me Big John my whole life. I even went to fat camp."

"Oh, I am so sorry."

"It's okay, babe. Let's eat. This is good food. Food that feeds the soul."

Preecha claimed, "You will never get fat eating my food, John. Most Thai people are skinny."

"That's good to know. I need food I can enjoy and still feel good about eating."

The three ate into the night and laughed as they shared stories about their lives. After they finished, Angela drove John home, dropping him off in the canyon. Before he got out, they kissed in the car and she thanked him for her ear— and for healing her heart, too.

14

That night, John lay in bed, wondering how best to apply his strange new gift. Should he go into medicine and secretly help patients? He didn't want to tell everyone he was helping them. For one, the word would spread quickly, and he would become famous in a bad way. He might even be locked up. He had wondered before if telepathic people got locked up. Certainly, people who saw buzzards turn into mystical beings in the woods could get sent away to somewhere. He wasn't about to share that with just anybody. He had confided in Angela, but she was a spiritual person. She understood. But could he tell his mom about it? She was nice and had her spiritual moments, but she would freak out if he told her the white wolf was his guide now. As for healing people, he didn't want the sense of false pride and inflated ego that was sure to accompany a constant stream of people thanking him and saying how great he was for helping them. He knew that if people knew he had cured them of a serious disease, they would never leave him alone with their gratitude, and he couldn't handle that. Maybe the old him would have reveled in it, but now being so slender and so adored by everyone had burnt out his desire for attention.

Now he wanted anonymity with his new gift. Where would he start? He was fifteen, and his whole life was before him. He could volunteer after school at a pet clinic. That seemed like a good place to start.

At school, John did his best to blend in, even though he was *the hottest thing on campus*, as one girl told him.

At school, Mike and Chris now avoided him. One day he tried telling them about Angela, but they couldn't understand why he no longer wanted to be with other hot girls at their school. He was, after all, one of the most popular guys on campus now and they wanted to be cool like him too.

One day Maggie had stopped John in the hall as he was walking by one day after class.

"I miss seeing you around, John. Where have you been lately?" she flirted with him, twirling her blonde locks with her finger.

"I have been busy, Maggie—see ya," he said and walked off down the hall. She slammed her locker and scowled.

His flippant lack of interest in her and other girls only made them like him even more.

One Thursday in biology class after lunch, John's teacher, Mr. Davis, was writing on the chalkboard. In the back, some disruptive kids were blowing spitballs at everyone. John dreaded this class because Maggie was in it. The thought that he ever saw anything in that shallow girl beyond a nice pair of legs and a gorgeous smile completely befuddled him. She played with the end of her pen in her mouth through most of the class and would look at him out of the side of her eyes from time to time.

Mr. Davis asked who knew where the mitochondria were located, and a lanky awkward guy with too many pimples named Shep raised his hand. At that moment, Mr. Davis's face turned blue and he fell to the floor with a loud thud. Members of the class swarmed the front of the room, asking if he was okay.

"I can't breathe," he wheezed.

John worked his way in, getting right next to Davis's side, where he gently placed his hand over his teacher's chest, pretending to be checking his breathing. One of the students raced out the door to get help. There was no change in Davis's condition, though.

John had been holding his hand on Davis's chest for a few minutes and it was starting to seem strange to everyone who couldn't figure out what he was doing or why. Davis's condition didn't budge; in fact, he was turning bluer.

The faculty member next door finally swung open the door and came to Davis's aid. She had called an ambulance and they would be arriving any minute.

Five minutes later, Davis was strapped in a stretcher and wheeled out of the high school front doors. John watched in total dismay as the ambulance drove off.

He was shocked. *What happened?* His miracle hands hadn't worked. He couldn't help, and he didn't know why. Why would it work sometimes and not others?

When class let out, John wanted to eat. The lust for a pound-of-cheeseburger-and-French-fry hangover was on his mind. He could actually taste the salt of the fries on the tip of his tongue. But he decided to go see Angela instead. It's what his heart wanted. He texted her and she picked him up on the way home. That night, they walked on the sandy beach and made out under the California stars, while she comforted him over his woes of the day.

A few days passed. John kept wondering about his ability. He wanted to try it again. Had he lost it? He didn't think so. Something told him it only worked in certain cases. He needed to ask the gypsy, though he felt that finding her in the desert again might be out of his reach. After school, he would go to see her. The old gypsy didn't even take appointments. It was a see as you go arrangement, but sessions were usually quick, ten minutes or so.

At Madame's, John waited for three people ahead of him to see the gypsy, which took over thirty minutes. When he entered the dark, musky room, Madame was wearing a green robe and spoke to him briskly, "Good to see you again, John."

"You too, Madame—listen I need to know about this gift you bestowed on me. It only works sometime, and I don't understand it."

"So, use it when you can, and when you can't, don't worry about it."

"But I want to help everyone. I must help everyone get well."

"No one can help everyone, John. Some people aren't meant to be well. Maybe they are meant to have a spiritual illness because they need to learn some lesson. That is for God to know, not for you and me to decide." She paused, shuffling her tarot cards. "Big John wanting to play God again, I see. How did that work with Maggie May?"

"Okay, you're right. Maggie was totally wrong for me. She

is an imbecile. I don't even like her anymore, and now she's crazy about me. I couldn't care less. But I need to understand how to use this gift you gave me!"

"You're going to have to relax into it. There's nothing to do and nowhere to go. Stay put and see what happens. When the time comes, your gift will come in handy. It's greater than you know."

15

On a foggy Saturday morning, John taxied to Santa Monica Memorial Hospital, where he entered Mr. Davis's room to find his teacher's health improved but still delicate.

"Hi Mr. Davis—how are you doing?" John asked, sitting beside his bed.

"Oh, hey John," Davis said weakly. "I am better today. Doctors said I have severe asthma and COPD, and I just had a severe asthma attack."

"Oh really, I am sorry to hear that."

"Yeah, life has been difficult lately since Betty, my wife, died of cancer. Some days, I don't know if I want to live anymore."

"I understand. Well hang in there, we need you at Santa Monica High; the kids look up to you. Stay strong."

"Hey, I have been meaning to ask you, how did you lose all that weight so fast? You look great now."

John laughed, "Just eating baby carrots and exercising I guess."

"Oh yeah? That's a testament to your willpower, buddy."

"Thanks. Hey, I gotta run Mr. Davis, but I am glad you are doing better now."

16

Over the next few weeks, John placed his hands on everyone and everything he encountered that was not well. He cured one woman of breast cancer and another of heart disease. His electric razor broke and he even fixed it, just by channeling energy into it through his palms. The more he used his gift, the more he understood it. Everything was energy at some level. He had always been good at science, and he understood that he was simply able to place a new higher frequency of energy through his hands into the living thing or object he was working on.

He was careful to never tell anyone what he was doing because he was afraid they would make him into some kind of strange hero. These days, John rarely ever saw Mike and Chris, instead hanging out alone or with Angela. She understood him, and he felt he now needed time to be silent and explore his new gift. He started reading a lot about healers and mystics, and he began to understand things that normal teenagers couldn't know.

One day, he and Angela were on the Third Street Promenade when they came upon a young crippled boy taking donations for a special operation he needed. John approached him and placed his left hand on the boy's shoulder and his right palm on his chest; all the while, the boy's mother watched on.

"What are you doing to my son?"

"One moment ma'am, I am just channeling a little healing energy to him, that's all."

After a minute, the boy suddenly stood up and began to dance in the middle of the breezeway.

"I am cured! It's a miracle! My God, *I can walk!*" the boy shouted with his hands up in the air.

Tears of joy streamed down his mother's cheeks as she ran up to John and squeezed him.

"You cured my son. I don't know what you did or who you are, but you cured my son."

"No ma'am, it's not me, it's just the energy. You're welcome, though."

And then John noticed that a crowd had gathered and that a teenage girl had been filming the whole episode on her phone. Everyone started to come up to John and touch him and hug him; grabbing Angela's hand, he pushed away through the crowd. They jetted off down a back alley. Many from the crowd ran to follow them.

John and Angela wound their way through back alleys and side streets, the mob hot on their tails. They saw their chance and ducked behind a large dumpster; the crowd swarmed by. The two had managed to escape, but it was too late—John's ability to cure people had been uncovered. The episode was later placed on YouTube and got a hundred million views by the end of the day. Every major news channel picked up the story and all the reporters were trying to find out who the mystery boy was who could heal cripples with his hands.

17

In the Techtonic offices outside of Palo Alto, Dexter Wade saw the news about the young crippled boy in Santa Monica the morning after it happened, on his eighty-inch curved black television. He grinned mischievously with his hands on his Empire-style antique mahogany desk. He cut off the tip of a fifteen-year-old aged Ghurka cigar and smelled it carefully before lighting it. He smoked the cigar slowly while watching the YouTube video on repeat.

Whoever that handsome young man was had to be the answer to all of Dexter's problems. Dexter was dead from the waist down due to a mountain climbing accident. Fifteen years ago, the young billionaire who had made a fortune pioneering a new kind of breast implant that didn't use silicone was mountain climbing when his belayer accidentally let slip the rope in his hand. Dexter fell fifty feet and landed on hard rock. He had stolen the breast implant formula from a college friend and felt the accident was a cruel punishment by the universe for his deceit. He had spent every waking hour since that bleak day searching the world over for a cure to his paralysis. No one in the medical field knew anything—early on he had even taken his private jet down to Panama to receive stem cell IVs that did nothing for him. Lately, he was looking for some kind of miracle worker—a shaman—as he had exhausted all alternatives. And this teenager in Los Angeles could be his answer. Lucas, Dex's assistant who looked more like a high school football coach than a Fortune 500 employee, walked in.

"Hey Dex, what's new today, boss?"

"Nothing much, but have you seen the news out of LA?"

"No, not yet," Lucas answered, his hands on his hips.

"Some paralyzed boy was cured by a teenager who laid his hands on him. Happened in front of everyone." Dex took a long, slow drag on the cigar.

"Really, no kidding?"

"Yeah ... what do you think it would take to get our hands on that boy, Lucas?"

"I don't know boss, but let me try to contact him."

"Sounds like a plan."

An hour later, Luke and John were talking on the phone by way of John's dad, who was impressed by the Fortune 500 company owner's interest in his only son. John's mother, on the other hand, was cautious about the whole thing. Prone to anxiety, she regarded this interest in her son to be strange and dangerous. John lounged in his recliner in his bedroom with Rocky in his lap.

"So, what would it take to get you to come up to Palo Alto and work on my paralyzed boss, Dexter, as soon as possible? You have a real gift, John. The world has seen that now. And

Dexter is paralyzed from the waist down. You could help him, you know."

"I am sorry mister, but I am just a teenager. Besides, no way my mom would let me go. I am also being chased by reporters, now that everyone in Los Angeles knows who I am."

"What would your mom say if we paid you a lot of money—how does a quarter of a million dollars sound?"

"Sounds like a miracle to me. I will ask her. One moment, let me dial her in...."

The phone rang three times and Susan answered.

"Hello?" she said, her sweet voice a little nervous.

"Hey mom, it's John."

"Hey, what's going on?

"Mom, I have Lucas Luther from Techtonic on the phone. He wants to ask you something."

"Sure—hello, Mr. Luther."

"Hey Mrs. Hoover, I work for Dexter Wade, the owner of Techtonic."

"Oh really, that's nice. What are you calling about?"

"We wanted to see if your son might be able to travel up to Palo Alto to see Dexter and work his magic on his legs. He is paralyzed from the waist down. We would compensate your family to the tune of $250,000 dollars. We will fly your whole family up here."

"Really? Wow, that's a lot of money. But go to Palo Alto? No, I don't think so. Why doesn't Dexter just fly some private plane down to LA and we can bring John to him?"

"He can't fly anymore. It's too hard on his body."

"Oh, well I am sorry, but we have to decline. We are just

worried sick about him with this video going around. Thanks, though." At that, she hung up.

"You see, Lucas? No way my mom will allow it," John said and hung up the phone.

Lucas strolled back into Dexter's office, biting his tongue. He relayed the news to his boss, who was prone to temper tantrums when his way wasn't met.

"Is that so," Dexter said upon hearing the news.

"I could pay some goons to kidnap the little dude and bring him to the lab."

"Do it. And Lucas?"

"Yes boss."

"Don't tell me about it until he's here."

"You got it."

Dexter spun his chair around and looked out the window before blowing a chimney cloud of dark Maduro smoke and squinting his beady little eyes out toward the horizon.

ngela had called John and said she would come over in thirty minutes. When she arrived, they went upstairs to unwind. John was worried now. Everyone had seen that stupid video and his parents and him had spent the afternoon discussing how to deal with the news and reporters. John checked the views on YouTube, which had soared to 900 million. "The Cure," as everyone was calling it, was officially a global phenomenon. If people believed John could cure ailments with his hands, they would come for him—they would want his power. It scared him. His phone rang again; he looked down—thirty-six missed calls. Eight of those were from Maggie. At that moment, she texted him a photo of herself in a very skimpy thong bikini. He deleted it quickly.

He walked over to the drawing of his new body and ripped it to shreds, throwing it in the trash. He sat next to Angela and gripped her hand.

"What are we going to do, John? This is bad," Angela said.

"I know, I just need to think."

"We could say it was all a big misunderstanding and you just mess around with a little reiki, that's all."

"Yes, we could."

He flipped the news on, and Mrs. Wong, a Chinese woman John had touched last week, was being interviewed. She had previously suffered with Lou Gehrig's disease and detailed to the reporter how all her symptoms had disappeared after the teenager had placed his hands on her. Then the screen shifted to the man whose Pekingese, Yahoo, had been restored to health from stage four cancer after John had touched her.

"Oh no, I'm screwed, Angela! These stories are all over the news. Everyone knows. They are saying my name. The reporters will be pulling up any minute. Can I stay at your house tonight until I figure things out?"

"Sure, let's go," she said. "Pack a bag."

"Okay," John said and started quickly throwing clothes into a suitcase.

They raced outside to her Prius and hit the road to Malibu. Relaxing in the silver bullet trailer, Angela brewed a fresh pot of coffee and prepared some eggs over easy. John was hungry like he used to be, but he knew the consequences of feasting and didn't allow the temptation to take over.

19

B axter William's black leather driving gloves gripped the tan Porsche Cayenne's steering wheel as he drove south from Palo Alto down US Highway 1. He'd left town the moment Lucas called him. The pistol sat in his passenger seat, loaded, with a silencer already screwed onto it. He was going to pick up Big John and bring him back to Dexter's laboratory. He had already been paid half the money up front: one million dollars in unmarked bills. He laughed at the thought of the job, kidnapping a teenager who could cure people. Maybe he could cure his eyesight and Baxter could throw away his glasses for once and all. That would be nice.

He sped down the interstate and was half the distance to LA. Dexter's hacker, whom he used to look into companies sometimes, had found John's address. The sooner Baxter got there, the better. He had seen the kid on the news—he looked strong. Not strong enough. Baxter could deliver a brutal beating if it came to that but that would maybe damage the goods for the healing. Perhaps he would just rough him up a little bit.

20

Angela and John laid together on her bed. John thought he was in heaven with this lovely Thai woman. He kissed her on the neck. And they talked until the sun came up.

The next morning was Sunday, thankfully, and the two walked down the Malibu beach. No one was out, but John wore a hoodie over his head and gold aviator sunglasses to disguise himself just in case.

Pelicans flew high over their heads, and a nice cold LA breeze howled off the Pacific. The two sat in silence for a while before heading back to the Airstream.

Preecha called Angela and asked if she had seen the breaking news about John. She replied she had not but would turn on the television, and then hung up.

John's dad kept calling, but John didn't answer. His dad texted that the reporters had arrived by the hundreds at their house. John texted back that he was hiding for a few days to avoid the fame. But his dad demanded to know where he was.

"I am in Malibu," John texted, "but I can't tell you where. Not now. It's not safe."

"Some girl named Maggie is here, and she keeps telling all the reporters she is your girlfriend."

"That's not true—tell her to go away."

His father told him he loved him and they agreed to talk again soon.

"What should we do, John? Where should we go?" Angela asked.

"We have to get away from the city—there are too many people here."

"We could go up to Big Sur for the weekend; no one's ever there."

"Okay. I am rich now from all these modeling gigs, so I can pay for a hotel no problem, but I can't tell my mom. She will freak out. She wouldn't even let me go to Palo Alto to work on this paralyzed guy for a quarter of a million dollars!" he said, and paused. "Pack a bag baby, let's get moving. Leave a note for your father and tell him not to worry."

21

Baxter approached the Santa Monica canyon address the hacker had texted him. A few news vans were still camped out in front of the house, but most had left after John failed to appear.

Baxter parked up the hill and made his way down the steep incline into the Hoovers' backyard. He drew his gun as he stealthily crept toward the back door. It was locked. He looked for an open window and found one, lifted it, and crawled in.

In the living room, Baxter found the Hoovers huddled around the television, waiting for news about their son's whereabouts. Aiming the gun at them, he demanded to know where their son was.

"He's gone! We don't know where he is," Susan replied.

Baxter grabbed Henry's cell phone and looked at the texts.

"Where are you Big John Hoover. Are you still in the city?" he said, laughing a cruel squall. Going through

Henry's texts, he remarked, "He's in Malibu, I see. So, who does he know in Malibu?" Bax pressed John's parents, frightened beyond belief.

"We don't know, we let him come and go as he pleases. We aren't strict parents."

Baxter smashed his hand into the grandfather clock in the living room. The cuckoo bird popped out on its spring, making a crow. He took John's parents' phones and exited out the back door.

With no phones, the Hoovers couldn't call the police, but they raced to the reporters out front and told them what had happened.

22

Dexter picked up the phone and Baxter was on the other end.

"I don't know where the boy is, but I know he's in Malibu. I have his parents' cells, but he won't answer them. The little pea brain."

"Okay, let me call the hacker and track the boy's phone. That's all we can do now."

Dexter called Brian Smith, his hacker. In Palo Alto, hackers were a dime a dozen. Brian was an out-of-work cyber-security specialist with a walrus moustache who resembled Captain Kangaroo. He had gotten fired for doing hash on his last job. Dex instructed Brian to start tracking John Hoover's phone. Once the hack was underway, Dex notified Baxter to wait for the activation from Brian.

23

Baxter had used Brian's live map application before. He pulled it up while he waited for the hacker to send John's whereabouts.

In a few minutes, the map starting beeping with a neon green dot that was traveling up route one, leaving Los Angeles county, heading toward Santa Barbara.

"Oh, they're on the move."

Baxter sped his Porsche out of LA, racing as fast as he could without getting noticed by the cops.

24

Angela and John were having fun listening to music and pretending the vibe surrounding them was less serious than before. What could they do about it, anyway?

"Have you ever been to Big Sur?" she asked him.

"Oh yeah, we used to go every summer. I love it there. My favorite thing is watching the hawks circle the mountains."

"I love that too. I used to see them there myself," she said, and paused. "You know my mom is from that area."

"Really? Was she Thai also, like Preecha?"

"No, she was Native American of the Esselen tribe. "

"Oh, that's amazing. I bet you loved her with all your heart."

"Yes—you know, she was a healer like you. People said she could cure many illnesses, but she used medicinal herbs."

"Really? Wow, that's so interesting. I wish I could have

known her," he replied, and waited a moment, looking out the window in contemplation.

"You would have loved her."

"I am sure," he paused. "You know, the gypsy woman told me my path was the way of the white wolf now—that the white wolf would be my guide. I wonder what that means?"

"I don't know, but maybe we'll see one up north."

"Maybe so. I hope so."

When the two stopped at a rustic gas station in Santa Barbara, a buzzard landed on the roof of the Prius. John was dumbfounded. He gave it some of his ice cream cone; after it ate, it flew off north—in the direction of Big Sur. John sensed that the bird was a sign they needed to keep moving. Danger could be close behind them.

25

The two lovers snaked up the scenic Highway 1. A low, earthy fog crept over the top of the mountains.

By about 3 a.m. or so, they had made it into the heart of the Big Sur canyon, stopping at a series of log cabins to their left. A shimmering light flickered in the main office. John started to go in, but Angela stopped him.

"Let me—you'll be recognized."

She went in and, using her most adult voice, booked them a cabin by the creek. The inquisitive night innkeeper asked for her ID, and she produced the New York State fake she'd had laser cut by a kid at Malibu High. It said she was twenty-one. She used the card to help her get into clubs and buy the occasional daiquiri. She felt less guilty about it now that it was helping to save her boyfriend's life.

The two walked to the romantic little cabin on the creek; John snuck a kiss as they entered. It was cold, so he threw some seasoned cut logs on the fire and lit them ablaze.

He boiled them some hot cocoa that the inn had provided, then wrapped Angela in a red and blue checkered flannel blanket and they sat by the fire, staring into the flames.

"It's so cozy in here, I love it. Let's have a house here one day just like this."

"Okay babe, sounds good to me."

As the logs died down, the two fell asleep right there by the fire, curled up in the blanket.

At 5 a.m., there was a loud banging on the door that startled John. But it turned out to just be the manager. He wanted Angela to move her car, which was in front of a service road entrance. She went and moved it, and she and John yawned and showered before getting dressed in some warmer northern California clothing.

They went out early to Nepenthe Beach, where they sank their toes in the sand. The ice-cold water, electric when it touched their feet, got into their bones. The horizon could barely be seen through the fog, but the sun was out and felt good on their faces.

John and Angela played in the sand some and picked up some interesting shells. They felt free, like no one would ever find them here in this paradise of sand and surf. As the two headed back to the car, a white wolf stood firmly at the edge of the bluff. When John pointed to it, the wolf cascaded down the hill and approached the two lovers playfully. John couldn't believe his eyes. The wolf's eyes shown with the intense blue of a gardenia and his fur was whiter than Christmas. The irises certainly didn't look natural and the wolf possessed a surreal aura standing there. John pet it slowly and the wolf tilted his head to embrace John's hand.

At that he ran off down the path towards the car and John and Angela chased after him, but he was nowhere to be found.

They headed to a spot serving breakfast up in the clouds with panoramic views of the ocean down below. The couple both craved eggs and bacon.

When their California sunrise specials arrived, they ate like two birds of a feather.

26

Baxter had entered Monterey county on the Central Coast from Highway 101. Since relocating to California from New Jersey, he had heard stories about how the slow, winding road through the mountains up Route 1 into Big Sur took hours, and figured he could cut some time by following the 101 into Monterey. He was now well on his way past the sleepy seaside village of Carmel and on to Big Sur, already exhausted by his tedious assignment. These little kids had cost him a whole two days of driving, and his neck was all sore now—he longed for a chiropractor to pop his spine.

Studying the map, he observed that the neon tracker had been in one spot for over an hour now, which stirred up some anxiety that John might leave soon and he would miss him. Up ahead, he noticed something standing in the middle of the road. It looked like a dog of some kind, but as he approached, he saw that it was a wolf as white as snow, standing sideways, staring him down with blue orbs for eyes.

He grabbed his gun as he slowed to a stop. No other cars were there. He slowly got out, pointing his pistol at the wolf the whole time.

"Go away, get gone!" he shouted.

But the wolf just stood there. Then, it took a step toward him and growled ferociously.

Frightened, Baxter jumped back in the Porsche and the wolf darted off into the woods. It had scared him too much to shoot it, and besides, a car was approaching from the other direction.

Five miles later, Baxter was pulling into the Big Sur cafe where John's cellphone sat, being tracked. Baxter backed the black Cayenne into a space.

After another long hour, Angela and John came frolicking out of the cafe, down the stone steps, and headed toward their car. Baxter watched them slowly. He knew what the boy looked like; the hoodie and shades didn't fool him.

The smiling couple got into their Prius and sped off. They headed up the coast to the town of Carmel for the day. The Cayenne tailed them, hanging back a distance.

When they pulled into the charming town by the sea, Bax followed them until they parked by the ocean. With only a few people by the water, Bax calculated it would be a good time to pick the boy up. He would leave the girl; she would only cause trouble.

Bax waited until Angela went to the bathroom and then crept up behind John, stuffed the nose of the pistol into his back, and told him to come along or die. Dumbstruck, John obeyed without much fight. Helpless, there was nothing he could do.

At the Cayenne, Bax tied John's hands in front of his body with a zip tie and crammed him in the back.

27

Angela came out and wandered around, calling John's name for over an hour, but he had vanished. She knew something was wrong. She called the police; a little while later, they showed up and she explained everything.

The police started tracking John's phone, but it only led them to a bathroom garbage can at a truck stop on the way out of town.

Stuffed like a sausage into the back of the luxury SUV, all of John's hunger returned. He was ravenous. He missed Angela and he didn't know who this strange bald guy was or what he wanted. He could have put away some In-N-Out animal style fries and taken a few double cheeseburgers to pound down. The thought now smelled like a greasy garbage can to him, and with great effort, he cast it away while devising a plan to escape.

A few hours later, the Cayenne whipped into Techtonic's lab in Silicon Valley. Dexter was already inside, waiting patiently for the healer to arrive whose name was now on the lips of every man, woman, and child in America.

When Bax opened the back door, John tried to kick him in the face but he missed, and Bax slugged him right across the jaw. Blood splattered across the inside of the trunk. That blow shut John up—he wasn't that tough. Sure, he had been in a few neighborhood scraps once or twice when someone said something racist he didn't agree with, but never a real bare-knuckle fistfight, and this assailant meant business.

Grabbing John by his sweatshirt hoodie, he pushed him around to a side door of Techtonic, where they entered a vast antiseptic room that stank of bleach and other cleansers. Animals of various types ran around in cages. There were rare monkeys from Africa and badgers and everything in between. Dexter had searched the natural world over for a cure to his paralysis.

"Is this the guy?" Dexter asked.

"Yep that's him."

"Bring him over here into the light. Let me get a good look at him. He looks different."

"Well I had to sock him because he tried to kick me."

"Oh, well, it's his hands we want, not his face. I am sure they still work."

"What do you want from me?" John asked, blood still running from the open cut on the side of his jaw where Bax's pirate skull ring had ripped into his flesh.

"I want your power in my legs. They haven't worked in years—and you can fix them, can't you?"

"I don't know. I can try I suppose, but I am not feeling very energetic after being kidnapped."

"Good," Dex said. "Cut him loose. Let him try to work his magic on these old worthless bones."

Bax cut the zip tie; John walked over to Dex, where he kneeled down beside his wheelchair. He placed his hands on Dex's knees and closed his eyes. He felt warmth surging through his palms as the tingling started.

After a few minutes, Dex's legs began to shake. John backed off and watched as Dex put one foot down on the shiny concrete floor and then the other, and then slowly leaned forward and stood up.

"It's alive," John said.

Dexter's astonishment stopped him from replying as he proceeded to walk across the room. He walked back to John, each step increasing in stamina and confidence.

"Oh my goodness," Baxter said, watching in amazement.

"It's a miracle. You, child, are a king—you are a God or something," Dexter exclaimed.

"You would like to believe that—that a person could be a God—but I am none of those things. It's just the energy in my hands; I just channel it. It's not magic or voodoo or anything more."

"Well, maybe it is. How about a job? Starting salary of five million a year. You work for me, doing this for others."

"I am sorry, I can't do that. It wouldn't be right."

"Take him away, go shoot him or something, I don't care about helping the world that much anyway, not anymore. And besides if we let him go, he will rat us out."

"Really? But boss, he's some kind of miracle boy," Baxter said.

"I don't care. Make it clean and do it now," instructed Dex.

Baxter led Big John into the alley behind Techtonic. Then he slugged John across the face with the butt of his gun and kicked him hard in the gut with his black alligator-skin cowboy boot.

"Do you want to die?" Bax asked, pointing the gun at John. Terrified, John anticipated the worst, shielding his face with his right hand.

At that moment, the sun began to shine blindingly bright.

"What the hell," Bax said.

A flock of birds flew overhead. Bax set the gun right against John's sweaty temple and squinted at him through the glare of the sunshine. But he couldn't pull the trigger. Not after what he had just seen. Baxter wasn't very spiritual, but the boy was some kind of special person—some kind of weird miracle worker. He wasn't going to be the one to send him to his death.

"Dammit. Go on now, run as fast as you can. Run like the wind, I tell you!"

John blinked twice, shook himself onto his two feet, and skirted off down the alley to freedom.

29

Angela's face was plastered on every news channel as she was being interviewed by all the major outlets. Her music had been downloaded and streamed millions of times, and her most recent YouTube video was now her most popular—"A Song to John" had been viewed over a billion times. She was an overnight sensation, and the record companies were banging down her door with multimillion-dollar offers and promises of the Grammys.

30

J ohn had no phone and couldn't call anyone. He flagged down the first car that approached on Highway 101, a golden Dodge Charger. The driver, a middle-sized German man named Stefan, stopped and wanted to know what had happened to him. Recognizing John, he praised him and agreed to take him all the way to Los Angeles on his way to San Diego.

That drive was the longest ride of John's life. His heart longed for Angela, and he wanted to see his parents, too— and to pet Rocky a good twenty times. When Stefan pulled in front of John's house, Angela's Prius was already parked in the driveway. The news vans were gone.

John thanked Stefan profusely and ran inside his house. His family hugged him, and he and Angela both cried as they embraced each other.

"What on earth happened to you, John? *Where were you?*" they all asked.

"That Techtonic guy I told you about paid some thug to

kidnap me so I could cure him. And he was going to have him shoot me mom!"

"Really? Oh my! How did you escape?" Angela asked, engulfed in his eyes.

"The kidnapper let me go after I cured his boss of paralysis."

"Oh wow, he must have changed his mind. You never know what some people are going to do, do you?" Susan asked.

"No, you really can't ever tell. Enough about me, tell me how you are doing."

"Well, we are good now that you're home," Susan said. "And Angela has some exciting news to report."

"Yes, guess what?" Angela said.

"What, what is it?" John smiled.

"I am rich now," she said, peering at him with those saucer black eyes.

"Really? How?"

"I just got an offer from Columbia Records to sign a contract for five million dollars."

"No way! That's amazing, girl."

"Yeah, I guess being famous has its benefits. Since your little trick on the promenade, everyone now knows who *we* are—*and* they know about my music."

John laughed out loud, then kissed her.

31

The next week, the happy couple bought a Moderne house for John's parents in Malibu near Preecha's home. She paid for a full security detail. John was homeschooled from then on, and most people ignored him after that day. Out of sight, out of mind. He began to channel his healing gift remotely through phone consults. He did as much as he could, and tried not to worry about healing the entire world, though his name was on the tongue of everyone from Iceland to South Africa.

Many sick people got cured, but many others didn't. And he never knew why. Why was Dexter able to be cured? A bad man—a billionaire criminal—and Mr. Davis was still sick? It was baffling to John, but he didn't need to know. It was enough to share what he could of his gifts with humanity— everyone getting lost in the mystery of life, all together. Dexter never followed up because he was now afraid of John. He had become scared of what it meant to kill someone with such powers.

After many years, John and Angela married and moved to the mountains of Big Sur, where they built a small cabin in the woods. She built a recording studio on the property.

One day, John's white wolf showed up, skirting the perimeter just to say hello. John tried to coax it into staying as his pet, but it was too wild to be tamed. It ran on the wings of the wind and with the spirit of the forest. However, he would come to visit John everyday just about and their relationship grew like the stony Blue Oak tree roots all around the cabin, but he still lived free in the forest. And he knew some spirits were meant to be free—like his and Angela's. That was the meaning of the white wolf. His growth as a healer would come through this life close to nature, seeking unity with the woods and the earth transformed from a bad food junkie and appearance worshipper to a warrior along the way of the white wolf.

ABOUT THE AUTHOR

Duke Tate was born in Mississippi where he grew up surrounded by an age-old tradition of storytelling common to the deep South. He currently lives in Southeast Florida where he enjoys fishing, surfing, cooking Asian food and reading.

You can view his YouTube channel here and his author website here.

amazon.com/Duke-Tate

goodreads.com/9784192.Duke_Tate

facebook.com/duketateauthor

twitter.com/duke_tate

ALSO BY DUKE TATE

The Opaque Stones

Returning to Freedom: Breaking the Bonds of Chemical Sensitivities and Lyme Disease

The Alchemy of Architecture: Memories and Insights from Ken Tate

Coming Soon:

Ken Tate in Black and White

Gifts from a Guide: Life Hacks from a Spiritual Teacher

Life Lessons from a Blue Macaw: Learning to Live in the Now